"Keep it with y...
Use it wise[ly]
Help others whe[n]
you can."
Happy 2nd Baptism Day
Anniversary
Olin

We love you,
Oma & Boppa

MW00935563

As Baptismal
sponsor-You are
always in my daily
Prayers As you grow in H's word. Boppa

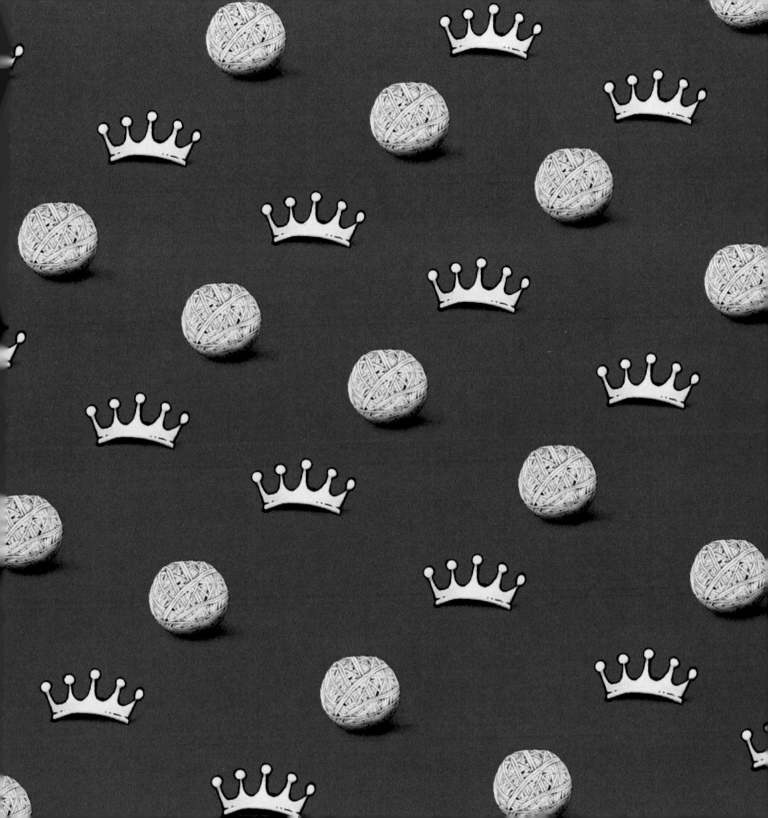

The Ballerina and The Bear

The STRING THING!

Written by David L. Burrier

Edited by Craig Biss

Illustrated by Anne Celesta Stevens

I dedicate my String Thing book to my faithful Heavenly Father and my Lord and Savior Jesus Christ! My dedication also extends to my family, including Karen Burrier, who has always provided inspiration, support and encouragement to my numerous ideas and ventures over the years and to my three grown children Joni (daughter), Brian (son), and Marcus (son) and my grandchildren, Miya, Isaiah, Maebry, June, Lainey, Norah and Jaxon.

The name, King Tovardana, pronounced Tov-are-donna, is a compilation of the letters of my parent's and sibling's names as indicated below.

<u>To</u>m Burrier (Brother), <u>Va</u>lerie Burrier Mormann (Sister), Leon<u>ard</u> Burrier (Father), <u>Dan</u>iel Burrier (Brother), Don<u>na</u> Burrier (Mother)

To God be the Glory!

-David Burrier

Presented to:

_____

From:

_____

Date:

_____

**"We are the Ballerina and the Bear Publishing,
and we are taking back family reading time since 2018."**

Once upon a time, in the Kingdom of Niceria, a message was sent throughout the land inviting all the children to come to the royal palace.

All who came would be rewarded with a special gift from King Tovardana himself.

Hundreds of children, along with their parents,
lined the road leading up to the majestic palace.
The King's mighty guards welcomed the children
as they arrived.

The children were escorted into the guest hall where they "patiently" waited.

The Royal Squire called upon them to enter the King's Throne Room.

"Marco?"

"Polo"

Upon entering the Throne Room, the children were amazed at what happened next. King Tovardana stepped down from the royal throne and humbly knelt before them, one at a time.

Placing a hand on their shoulder, King Tovardana,
looked each of them in the eyes and said,
"You are a very special member of our Kingdom."

King Tovardana presented each child with a roll of string, along with written instructions.

"Keep this roll of string with you at all times, use it wisely, and help others when you can."

Throughout the kingdom, each child obeyed the orders of the King and kept their roll of string by their side. Although they didn't fully understand why the king gave them string, they often reminded each other of the king's words of wisdom.

Keep this roll of string with you at all times, use it wisely, and help others when you can.

One day, something terrible happened. Someone had fallen into the Royal Well and was trapped deep inside. Villagers rushed to help and gathered around the opening of the well. The hole was so deep that they were unable to see who it was.

Villagers tried several ways to help rescue the trapped person, but nothing was working. The children kept their distance and watched as the adults tried to save the trapped person.

"Well, that didn't work…"

A little girl, named Faith, was watching from far away and slowly moved closer to the opening of the well. When Faith's parents saw she, too, was trying to help, their hearts grew warm.

"My ball of string might work."
"Has anyone tried to get them out?"
"There is nothing anyone can do!"

A couple villagers doubted Faith saying she was "too little" to help, but that did not stop her from trying.

Grabbing her roll of string, Faith began lowering it down the deep dark hole.

"Look at our little girl, she is so courageous!"

"Use it wisely and help others when I can."

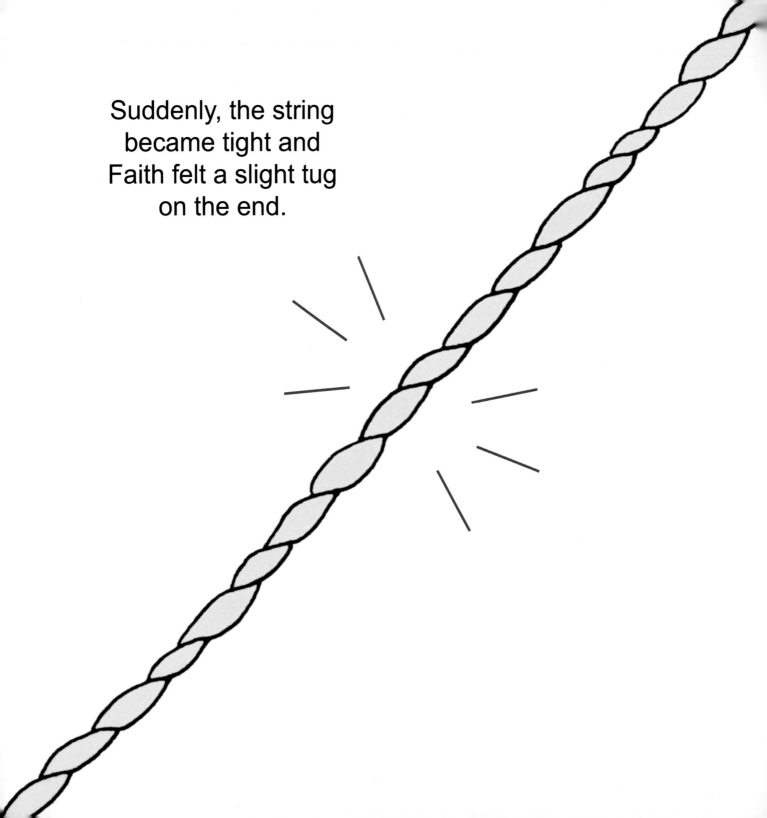

Suddenly, the string
became tight and
Faith felt a slight tug
on the end.

The villagers froze in amazement. They watched as Faith tried to lift the trapped person out of the well, but Faith's string was not strong enough.

Faith's friend, Hope, watched eagerly from the side. Hope remembered that she, too, had a roll of string. King Tovardana had told her to "Keep this roll of string with you at all times, use it wisely, and help others when you can."

Hope and Faith combined their rolls of string and lowered them down the hole. The adult villagers didn't know what to say because all their ideas had already failed. Faith's parents encouraged them to keep trying.

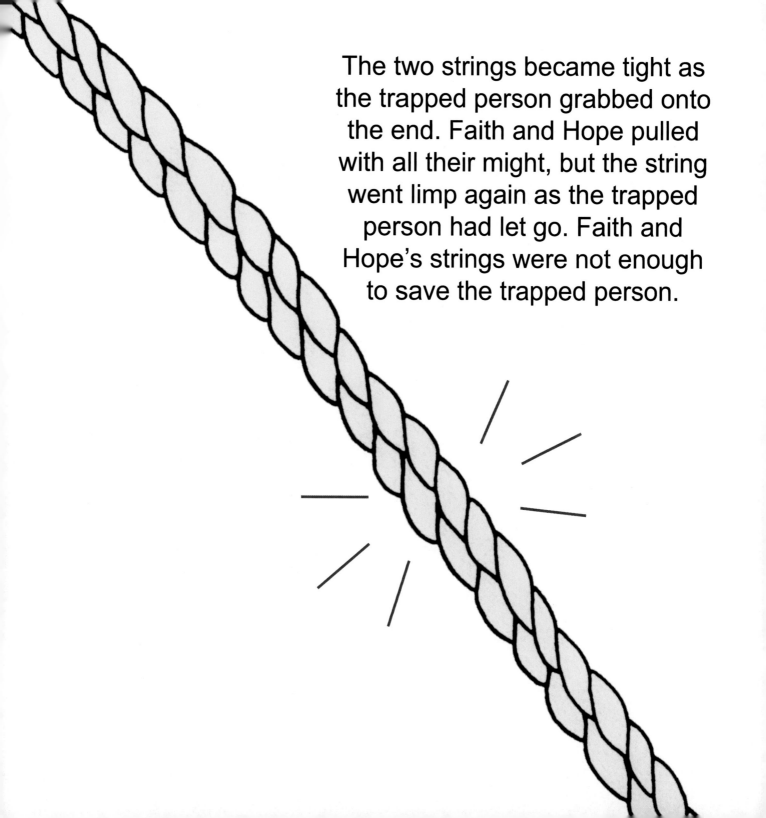

The two strings became tight as the trapped person grabbed onto the end. Faith and Hope pulled with all their might, but the string went limp again as the trapped person had let go. Faith and Hope's strings were not enough to save the trapped person.

A short and stocky young boy nicknamed, "Little Love", watched from a distance as Faith and Hope struggled to pull the trapped person from the well. Several children were playing games in the distance and Little Love waved at them to follow him to the Royal Well.

"We can help, King Tovardana gave all of us a roll of string, too!"

Before long, Little Love had gathered more than one hundred children. Each child carried their roll of string and had come to help. Faith, Hope, and Little Love tied a knot to combine all the strings together.

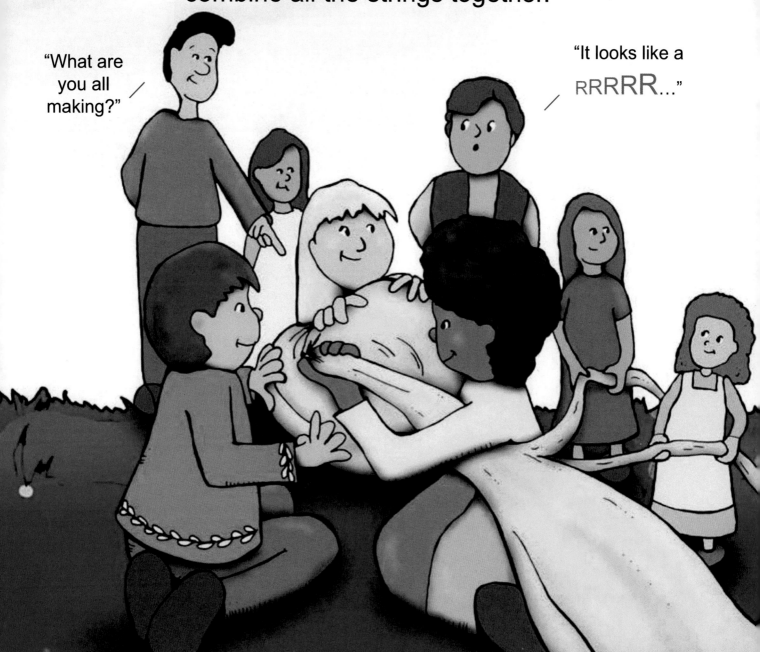

STRING

The String Thing was so large that all the children had to work together to lower it down the opening of the well.

Within a couple of seconds of the String Thing reaching the bottom of the well, there was a strong tug on the end of the string. Faith, Hope, and Little Love all started shouting...

Pull!

PULL!

Pull!

Eventually, the trapped person was freed!
Everyone cheered but looked at each other and wondered, "Who had they saved?"

"THE CHILDREN SAVED THE KING!"
shouted the villagers.

A few weeks later, the King gathered the whole Kingdom to present the String Thing Award saying,

"Let the story be told, far and wide, that I was trapped and alone, but now I am free! The String Thing Award is to remind us all that with Faith, Hope, and a Little Love, we are all able to do great things. We are better together and stronger when we use our gifts wisely by helping others when we can!

The news of the String Thing spread throughout the world. To this day, the String Thing is still celebrated and seen in a variety of ways.

The String Thing continues to be a symbol that when Faith, Hope, and a Little Love are together, then anything is possible.

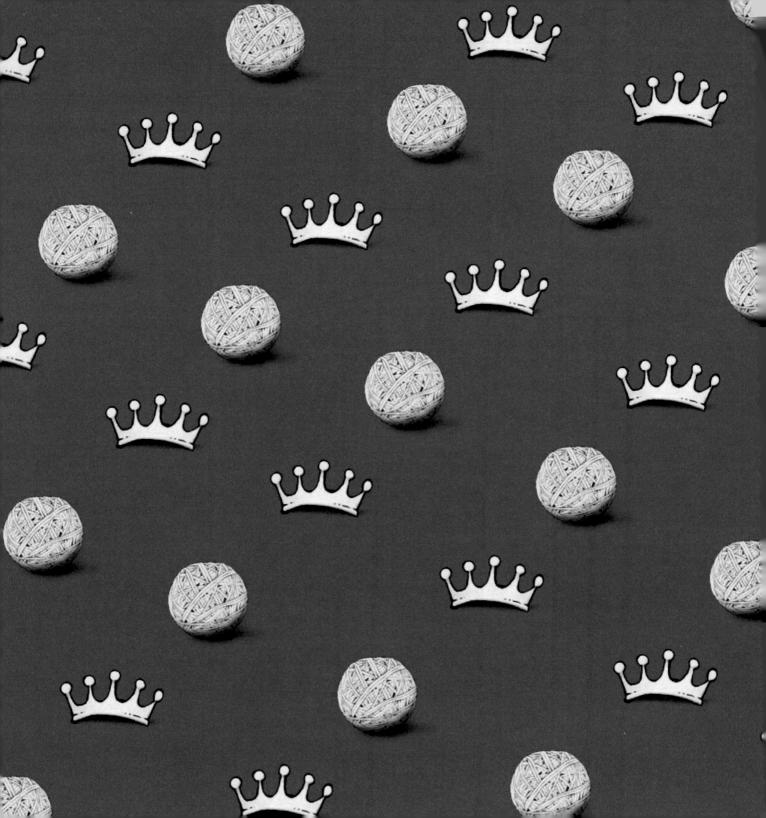

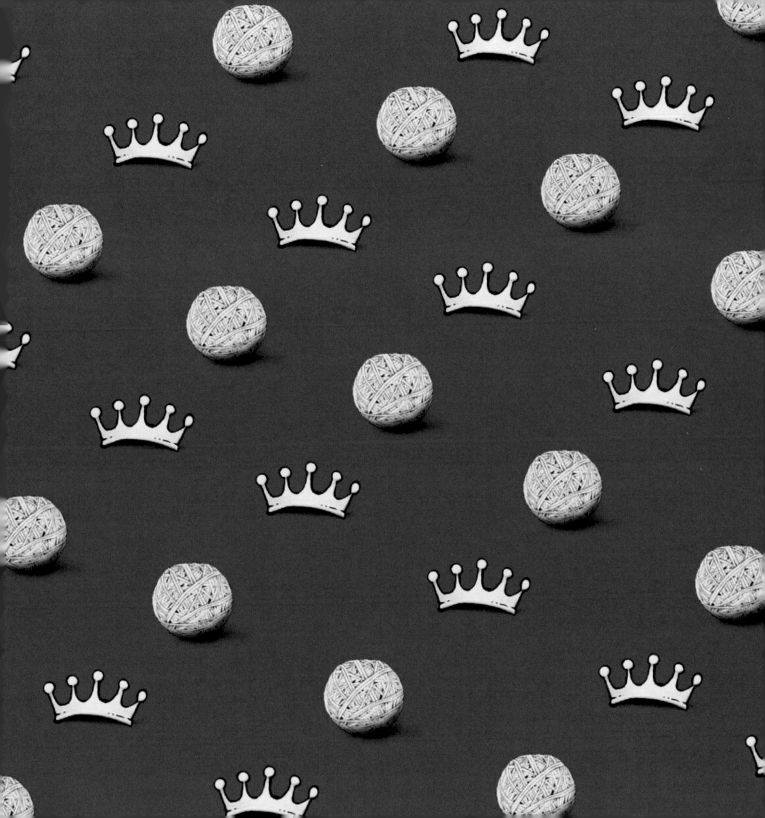

About the Author

David L. Burrier grew up on a farm in northeast Iowa where he recalls being inspired at a young age as he observed neighbors joining together to harvest the crops of a disabled farmer. That profound experience set the stage for David's life-long quest to create projects and organizations based on the premise that, "when we work together to help others, we strengthen ourselves."

David is a motivational/inspirational speaker, published author, poet, singer, songwriter and master storyteller.

He is the founder of I'VE BEEN THERE Ministries (IBTM) – a non-profit organization whose mission is to bring a message of hope to a hurting world. Many of his creations can be found on his website at www.ivebeenthereministries.com, where you can schedule him to speak at conventions, school assemblies, churches and other gatherings.

You can read David's daily messages of hope on the IBTM Facebook page at https://www.facebook.com/ivebeenthereministries/

Follow David on his personal Facebook page at https://www.facebook.com/david.burrier.56.

David says, "As our society has steadily moved toward isolationism, we have missed the opportunity to experience the joy of working together to help others."

More information about The String Thing book can be found at www.stringthingbook.com including scheduling David as your speaker or for book signing events.

An adult supplemental discussion group questionnaire is available in PDF for download at www.stringthingbook.com.

The String Thing Story
What Can it Teach Our Children?
Discussion Guide for Children led by Parents, Teachers & Other Adult Mentors

Use this optional questionnaire to facilitate a discussion with children.

1. Why did King Tovardana invite the children of Niceria to the palace?
2. What did the King tell the children to do with their roll of string?
3. Why do you think the little girl, named Faith, stepped up to help?
4. What were the instructions from the King that Faith remembered?
5. Do you think that Faith believed her single strand of string would really work?
6. Why didn't Faith give up trying to help save the person trapped in the well when she realized her string wasn't strong enough?
7. Why do you think the little girl, named Hope, stepped up to help Faith?
8. Why didn't Faith and Hope just give up trying when they realized that even their two combined strings were not strong enough to save the person trapped in the well?
9. What was the name of the little boy who stepped up to offer to help?
10. What did Little Love do?
11. Why did the many children come running to help?
12. What do you think it was like with all those children working together?
13. Why do you think some of the adults doubted that the silly looking String Thing would even work?
14. What do you think made the King the happiest?
15. How do you think that day changed the Kingdom of Niceria?
16. What lessons can we learn from The String Thing story? What does it teach us?
17. What does the following quote mean? "When we work together to help others, we strengthen ourselves."
18. What kind of gifts do you think you have?
19. Have you ever used your gifts or talents to help someone?
20. Have you ever been a part of a String Thing group of people who worked together to help someone in need?
21. What ideas could you come up with to create a String Thing group?
22. What will you think of whenever you see a tassel?
23. What was the instruction to the children when the King gave them their roll of string?

The Ballerina and The Bear

Leprechauns in Texas

Ballerina is gorgeous in her green dress, she shines like the Emerald Isle

Our young siblings prepare for the St. Patrick's Day Parade and a day filled with adventure. Ballerina and Bear make a wager. If Bear spots a leprechaun, then he wins. If not, then he must eat corned beef and cabbage.

Will Bear spot a leprechaun in time?

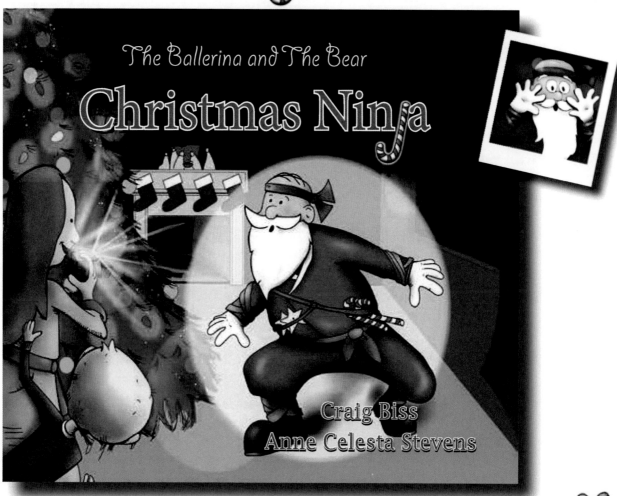

The String Thing Effect

One strand alone can pull lots of weight,
Though some think it can't, so they hesitate.

One never knows just how strong theirs could be,
And won't 'til they step out in front courageously.

Once they discover the strength they possess,
Belief in themselves builds their confidence.

Others will follow because, they can see hope,
They step forth in faith as they've watched other folks.

Hope is why people help others in need,
It's what people long for as most would concede.

Together they learn that stronger they'll be,
When many combine it's called synergy.

New meaning in life is what it will bring,
'Cause it's never the same once you've been in a String Thing.